This book belongs to...

_____

_____

_____

Pirates vs. Monsters
An original concept by author David Crosby
© David Crosby
Illustrated by Lee Cosgrove

First Published in the UK in 2020 by
MAVERICK ARTS PUBLISHING LTD

Studio 11, City Business Centre, 6 Brighton Road,
Horsham, West Sussex, RH13 5BB
© Maverick Arts Publishing Limited 2021
+44 (0)1403 256941

American edition published in 2021 by Maverick Arts Publishing, distributed in the United States and
Canada by Lerner Publishing Group Inc., 241 First Avenue North, Minneapolis, MN 55401 USA

ISBN 978-1-84886-708-6

Maverick
publishing
distributed by Lerner™

For George - D.C.
For Cara & Finn - L.C.

PIRATES vs.
MONSTERS

Written by David Crosby

Illustrated by Lee Cosgrove

Three pirates met up at the old Parrot's Head,
To brag about **monsters** they'd each left for dead.

They boasted and laughed and drank lots of grog...

...While in from the sea crept a **blanket of fog.**

The first pirate, **Hector**, was tall, strong and **bold**,

And the teeth in his mouth were a **glimmering gold**.

"The **Hockler**," he bellowed, "could soar through the sky,
And spit globs of **poison** straight into your eye,
How did I beat it? You'll say the mind boggles!"

"With an arrow, a bow and a good pair of **goggles!**"

The pirates all **cackled**, tears rolled from their eyes,
While a ship nearing port, held a **frightful** surprise.

The next pirate, **Sue**, was a fearsome old girl,
With a **patch** on her eye, and her hair in a **curl**.

"The **Crunk**," she spat, "was a two-headed beast,
While one head would sleep, the other would **feast**."

"How did I beat it? With my **sneaking** skills!

I sprinkled its grub, with **crushed sleeping pills!**"

They all stamped their feet, with **horrible glee...**

...Outside from the ship, came not one shape but **three**.

The last pirate, **George**, was round like an egg,
Under one of his knees, was a bright copper **peg**.

"The **Muncher**," he snarled,
"bites pirates on sight,
He **ate** my left leg but did not
get my right."

"How did I beat it? You're **desperate** to know!

I put pirate clothes on **a metal scarecrow!**"

They all laughed so hard that they fell to the floor...

...But their howls were drowned out by a **BANG** on the door!

The piano fell silent, replaced by a **SCREAM!**

Three **creatures** burst in, like a nightmarish dream!

Three **monsters** met up at the old Parrot's Head,
To brag about pirates they'd faced and had **fled**,
They boasted and laughed and got warm by the fire...

...But unlike the pirates, not one was a **LIAR!**